What's this page for?

It's called the endpaper, but it comes at the beginning.

Dedicated to my friend,
Dr. Dan (Medicine Man),
who provided me with the
opportunity to do less.

Published by Scholastic Press, an imprint of Scholastic Inc., Publishers since 1920.
SCHOLASTIC, SCHOLASTIC PRESS, and associated logos are
trademarks and/or registered trademarks of Scholastic Inc.

The Cat, the Dog, Little Red, the Exploding Eggs, the Wolf, and Grandma
was originally published in the UK by Frances Lincoln Ltd. in 2014 under the title
The Cat, the Dog, Little Red, the Exploding Eggs, the Wolf and Grandma's Wardrobe.

Library of Congress Cataloging-in-Publication Data Available

ISBN 978-0-545-69481-0

10 9 8 7 6 5 4 3 2 1   14 15 16 17 18

Printed in China
First US edition, September 2014

THE CAT, THE DOG, LITTLE RED, THE EXPLODING EGGS, THE WOLF, AND GRANDMA

Diane and Christyan Fox

Scholastic Press • New York

There was once a sweet little girl who lived with her father and mother in a pretty little cottage at the edge of the village.

She always wore a red cape with a hood, which suited her so well that everybody called her Little Red Riding Hood.

What's this?

It's a story about a little girl ··· who always wears a red cape with a hood.

COOL! I love stories
about superheroes.

What's her
special power?

She doesn't have
any special powers.

It's not that
kind of a story.

So, what
happens?

Well, one morning
her mother asked
Little Red Riding Hood
to take a basket of
eggs, butter, cake,
and sweets to her
grandmother.

So kindness is her special power? Does she hypnotize bad guys into being nice?

And what kind of candy?

Look, do you want to hear this story or not?

So where was I?

Little Red Riding Hood was on her way to Grandma's house when she met a wolf...

A WOLF! EXCELLENT!

They're always the bad guys in stories like this.

I bet she zaps him with her
KINDNESS RAY.

ZZZZ!!

She does <u>NOT</u> have a
KINDNESS RAY...

she has a basket of
eggs and butter and
cakes and sweets.

How does she fight
crime, then? Does she
have a cool kind of
flying gadget basket?

Are they
exploding eggs?

THERE'S **NO** KINDNESS RAY, **NO** FLYING BASKET, AND **NO** EXPLODING EGGS.

SHE'S JUST A SWEET LITTLE GIRL WITH TERRIBLE FASHION SENSE ON HER WAY TO SEE HER GRANDMOTHER.

OK, ok... so let's hear the rest of the story.

Well, the Wolf asked
Little Red Riding Hood
where she was going and
she said, "Grandma's house,"
so the Wolf said good-bye
and secretly headed
to Grandma's house...

Hang on...

why doesn't the
Wolfman try to
eat Hood Girl
then and there?

You're doing this
on purpose,
aren't you?
How should I
know why he
didn't eat her?

Hmm...
I wonder
why the Wolf
prefers
old ladies?

Anyway, the Wolf arrived at Grandma's cottage and saw the old lady lying in bed. She jumped up when she saw the Wolf, and locked herself in the closet.

I think the Wolf needs to think bigger if he's going to be a super-villain.

Maybe he could rob a bank on the way to Grandma's house?

Yes.

OK, so Grandma leaped up out of bed and locked herself in the closet to be safe.

Then the Wolf put on some of Grandma's clothes and climbed into the bed, waiting for Little Red Riding Hood to arrive.

Hang on...

so now you're saying he DOES want to eat her?

Yes... anyway, this is my favorite part. She arrived and said, "What big eyes you have, Grandma." And the Wolf replied, "All the better to see you with."

She's not very bright, is she? I mean, if there were a Wolf dressed up as MY grandma, I might have noticed right away.

...and Little Red Riding Hood said, "What a big nose you have, Grandma."

And the Wolf replied, "All the better to smell you with, my dear."

Let me see that book...

...And she said, "What big teeth you have, Grandma." And the Wolf said...

ALL THE BETTER TO EAT YOU UP!

YIKES!

But just at the last moment,
Little Red Riding Hood's
father arrived and

CHOPPED OFF THE WOLF'S HEAD WITH AN AXE!

GULP!

And they all
lived happily
ever after.

I'm not sure
that the Wolf
was very happy
in the end.

So let's see if I have this right.
The Red Hood is on her way to
help an old lady when she meets
the Wolfman. He has an evil plan.
He likes to dress up in girls' clothes
and eat people. He and Red have
a big battle, and Red's father
puts an end to Wolfie.

Well...
sort of...

It's not a very
nice story, is it?

Are you absolutely
sure this is a
children's book?

THAT'S IT!
I'm leaving.
Find your own
book to read.

Just one
last
question...

What?

Is Grandma
still in the
closet?

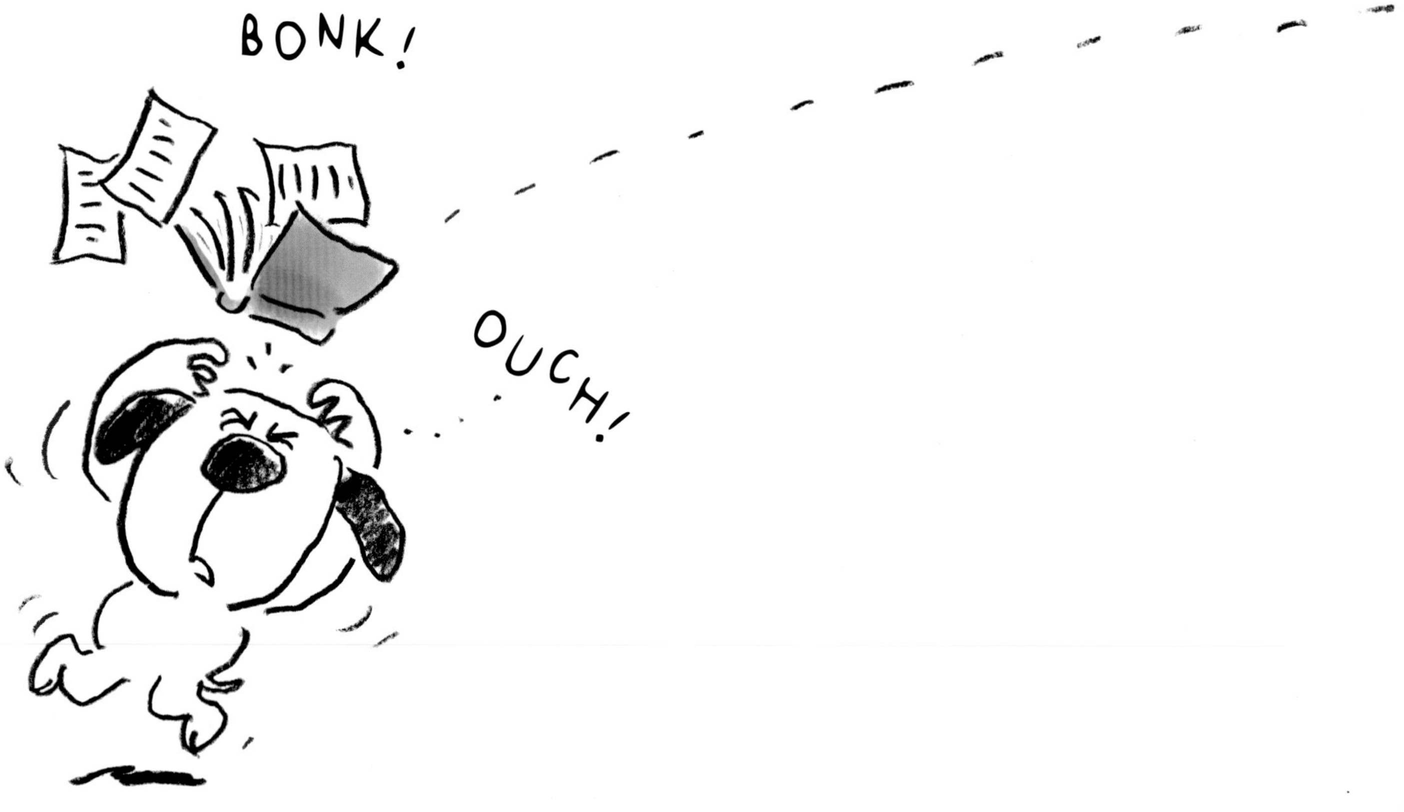
BONK!
OUCH!

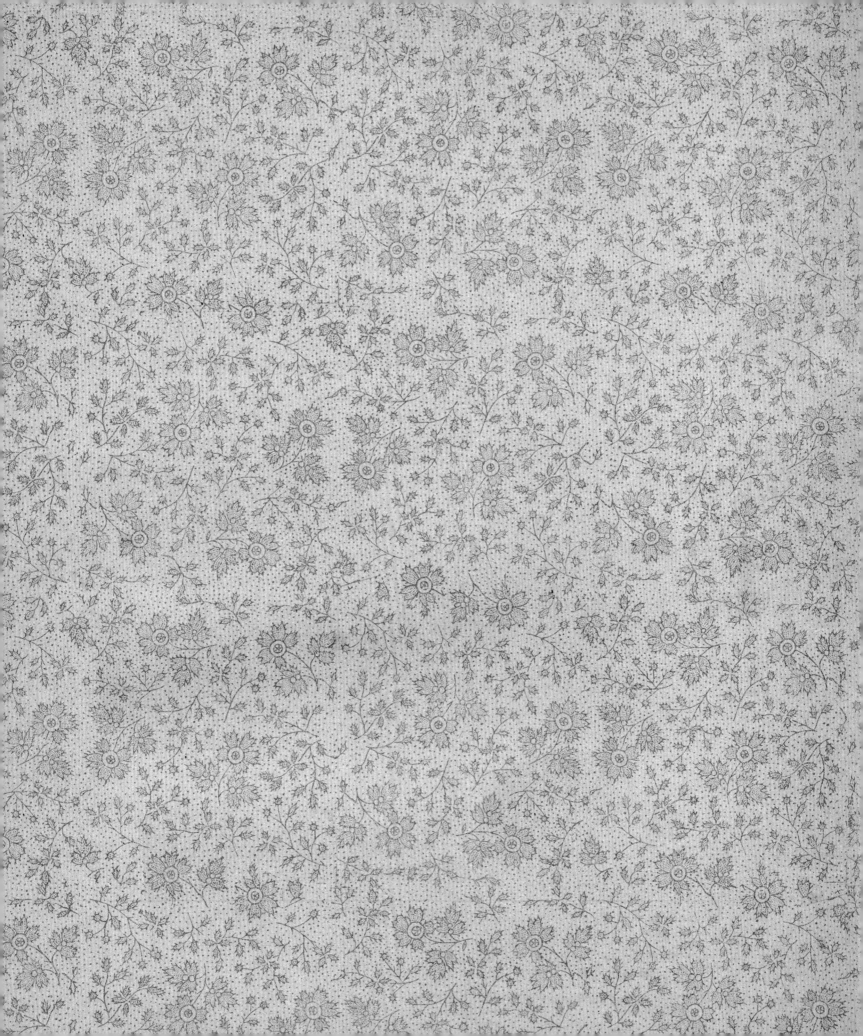